THE SECRET ROOM

BY H. TOWNSON

illustrated by Martin Salisbury

Librarian Reviewer
Kathleen Baxter
Children's Literature Consultant, formerly with Anoka County Library, MN
BA, College of Saint Catherine, St. Paul, MN
MA in Library Science, University of Minnesota, MN

Reading Consultant
Elizabeth Stedem
Educator/Consultant, Colorado Springs, CO
MA in Elementary Education, University of Denver, CO

STONE ARCH BOOKS
Minneapolis   San Diego

First published in the United States in 2006
by Stone Arch Books,
151 Good Counsel Drive, P.O. Box 669,
Mankato, Minnesota 56002.
www.stonearchbooks.com

Published by arrangement with
Barrington Stoke Ltd, Edinburgh.

Library of Congress Cataloging-in-Publication Data
Townson, Hazel.
The Secret Room / by H. Townson; illustrated by Martin Salisbury.
      p. cm. — (Pathway Books)
      Summary: When Adam enters a secret closet at his school, he is
transported through time to 1942, into the middle of a World War II air raid.
      ISBN-13: 978-1-59889-003-7 (hardcover)
      ISBN-10: 1-59889-003-4 (hardcover)
      ISBN-13: 978-1-59889-199-7 (paperback)
      ISBN-10: 1-59889-199-5 (paperback)
      [1. Time travel—Fiction. 2. Schools—Fiction. 3. World War,
1939–1945—Great Britain—Fiction. 4. London (England)—History—
Bombardment, 1940–1945—Fiction. 5. Great Britain—History—
1936–1945—Fiction.] I. Salisbury, Martin, ill. II. Title. III. Series.
PZ7.T6675Sec 2006
[Fic]—dc22   2005026583

Cover Illustratior: Brett Hawkins

1 2 3 4 5 6 11 10 09 08 07 06

Printed in the United States of America

Table of Contents

CHAPTER 1

The Key

Adam Belman was bored. He had just moved to Hope School in the middle of the school year. The work was less interesting than at his old school. The teachers here talked too much, and there was nothing to do.

They were learning about World War II, which Adam found really boring. In fact, he was half-asleep in the middle of the lesson.

Adam was thinking about nothing much when, suddenly, he had an idea. He woke up with a jump. He might have found the first clue to a puzzle!

Jade Green was the only person in his class who had shown any interest in him. She had told him that there was a secret room somewhere in the school. But no one had ever been able to find it.

Because he had nothing better to do, Adam spent his free time going around the school looking for a hidden door. Maybe if he found the secret room, it would win him some friends.

Adam hadn't found any clues until now.

In the middle of this boring lesson, he had an exciting idea.

The teacher, Mr. Evans, had put a huge, old key on his desk. The label hung over the desk, so Adam could read it: SUPPLY CLOSET. The label was Adam's first clue because no supply closet needed a key as big and as old as this one. And Hope School had just been remodeled.

That label could not be right. It must be a code for something else, like a secret room!

Adam Belman was wide awake now. His mind was racing. He must get that key right away.

Adam didn't hear a word of the lesson. At the end of class, Mr. Evans asked him to stay for a minute. This was Adam's big chance. As he talked with Mr. Evans, Adam leaned across the teacher's desk and slipped the key into his pocket.

There was a staff meeting that day after school. Adam could try out the key while the teachers were busy. The only bad thing that could happen was that Mrs. Yates, the custodian, might see him.

If she did, Adam would tell her he was looking for his lost gym uniform and didn't dare go home without it.

After school, Adam hid in the boys' bathroom. Then he crept past the staff room door to make sure that the meeting had begun. Yes, he could hear people talking.

Feeling safe, Adam went off to find the supply closet, which he knew was in a dark corner off the main hall. This end of the hall had a brown curtain in front of it. The folding lunch tables were kept behind it, with all the football and gym equipment. In fact, it was hard to get to the closet door at the back.

There was a huge keyhole in the door. The big key fit it perfectly. Adam looked back to make sure no one was watching. Then he turned the key and opened the door. A light came on in the small room as he walked inside.

Adam saw just what you would expect to see in a supply closet. There were shelves with pens, notebooks, and sets of books. There were boxes of tissues and rulers and bundles of pencils in boxes. Nothing strange at all. There wasn't another door in the wall and there was no secret panel.

Oh, well. It had been a good idea to try. Maybe he'd keep the key for a while to see if it fit somewhere else.

Adam was just about to leave when the door slammed shut behind him. The light went out. Then a key turned in the lock. Mrs. Yates must have seen the door was open and locked it with her own key.

It was a good thing Adam hadn't left his key in the door. It was still safe in his hand. No need to panic.

Adam waited a moment to give Mrs. Yates time to walk away. Then, feeling around in the dark, he found the keyhole and opened the door again. But now he did panic.

All the clutter behind the brown curtain was gone. The curtain was gone, too. The 6th grade art display, which had been hanging on the walls in the hall, was also gone.

All that was left on the walls were two posters from long ago. One said, "Dig for Victory" and the other "Careless Talk Costs Lives."

Adam stared, shocked and amazed. He began to notice other changes, too. Every window now had thick, black curtains instead of pretty, flowery ones. All the panes of glass were crisscrossed with strips of brown tape.

No one could have made all these changes in the short time Adam had been in the closet. Something very odd was happening — something very scary.

Had he found the secret room after all?

Chapter 2

A Siren Sounds

Adam just stood there. He could
not decide what to do. Should he step
back into the closet and try to get back
to where he'd come from? Or should
he explore this weird place, which
was both the same as the school hall,
and yet so different? This was his
big chance. He was sure to have an
amazing story to tell. Everyone would
want to hear it.

Before he could decide what to do, a girl ran into the hall. She saw him and called out, "Hurry up! The siren's gone off! Didn't you hear it?"

Adam was pleased to see that it was Jade Green. She was running down the hall very fast, carrying a coat and a cardboard box. For some odd reason, Jade wasn't wearing her school uniform. She had on a shabby dress and sweater.

Adam had never heard the siren before. When it went off, he thought it was the fire alarm. He didn't know what to do.

Jade grabbed his arm and dragged him off into the playground.

Neat lines of children were marching away from the school, across the playground, and down some steps into concrete shelters. Adam had never noticed these before.

None of the children wore uniforms. They all carried a coat and a cardboard box like Jade's.

Adam and Jade joined the end of one of the lines. They were soon sitting in a shelter along with thirty other children and two teachers. They sat on wooden benches in the cold, damp dugout. The floor was soft dirt. The teachers were holding up lamps and checking that the children were all there.

"Put your coats on! It's cold down here," ordered one teacher.

The other teacher asked Adam, "Where's your gas mask?"

"It's all right, sir. It's here!" Jade said.

She pulled out something from under the bench and put it on Adam's lap. It was a cardboard box on a string, like the one she and all the others were holding.

"Well, keep it with you," said the teacher. "Don't put it down where you might lose it!"

"Now remember not to ask for food or water until we've been here at least half an hour," he went on. "And, Jade, I think it's your turn to start the singing today."

The children started with a song Adam didn't know. He looked around him. He saw that one of the boys had a jug of water and some paper cups, and a girl was holding a large cookie tin.

Were they going to stay here all night? And if so, was this the only food and drink they'd get?

Adam shivered. He didn't like it down here. It smelled damp and nasty, and the wooden bench was hard. "How long do we have to stay here?" he asked Jade between songs.

"Until the 'all clear,' of course."

"When will that be?" asked Adam.

"Who knows?" said Jade. "Anyway, it's not all bad. We've missed the spelling test today."

Adam didn't know about the spelling test, but school must be over for the day. He looked at his watch. It had stopped at 3:45 p.m., the exact time he had walked into the closet.

None of this made any sense, but as long as Jade was there he felt everything would be all right. Adam wasn't used to this strange new school yet, but Jade had been here all her life. She would look after him.

Then the droning noises in the air above them turned into one huge crash! Adam put his hands over his ears. Even down here, deep in the concrete bunker, he could feel the earth shaking all around him. It was weird. Everyone looked tense. Two girls were hugging each other and one of the boys began to cry. A teacher put an arm around him.

What was going on? What had exploded so loudly? Suddenly, Adam understood that this was an air raid.

Now he was really scared. He gripped Jade's arm, but she grinned and said, "It's okay, that one didn't sound too close."

At last, after more thuds and bangs, a long wail from the siren gave the 'all clear.'

Everyone cheered.

One of the teachers looked outside, then gave the signal to go. The children marched up the steps and into the playground. It had been exciting, but they were glad it was over. It was good to move around and get warm again. But in the distance, they could see a huge fire burning up a local factory, a factory that Adam hadn't noticed was there before.

Adam was about to panic. He didn't like this. Was he going crazy?

As soon as he could, he slipped away from the others and ran back into the hall. With shaking hands he pushed the key into the supply closet lock.

He opened the door and hurried in. This time he locked the door on the inside.

The light went out and he was in the dark. He counted slowly up to 50. Then he turned the key again and stepped out into the hall. What would he see?

He cried out with relief.

Everything was the same as it had been before he went into the closet. The brown curtain was there with all the clutter piled behind it. The flowery curtains were back in the windows, and the 6th grade art display was up on the walls again. Even the hands of his watch had started to move again.

Was there some weird magic going on? Had he fallen asleep in there and just had a bad dream? It was too weird to be real. He better put the key back on the teacher's desk and try to forget all about it.

Adam was just going to slip the key back into his pocket, when he felt something hanging down his back. It was a cardboard box on a piece of string — the box with the gas mask that Jade had given him!

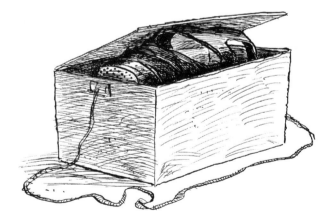

Chapter 3

Drastic Changes

Adam went back to Aunt Laura's
and Uncle Tim's house where he had
been staying for the last couple of
weeks while both his parents were in
the hospital. Aunt Laura and Uncle
Tim had been taking care of him since
his family had a car accident.

Adam escaped with only a few cuts.
His dad had broken both of his legs.
His mom was not too bad but was kept
in the hospital for another reason.

His mom was going to have a baby soon, and the doctors needed to be sure she was all right.

Uncle Tim had told Adam that everything would be fine. Adam would soon go back to live with his own family. Until then, he should try not to worry. He should not mind having a different home and school for a while.

But Adam did worry.

How badly were his parents hurt?

Adam still didn't know exactly what had happened. He hadn't been able to visit them either. Maybe the unborn baby was hurt, and he would never have the new brother or sister he was looking forward to.

It might be selfish of him to think this way, but it bothered Adam that he had to leave all his friends, his school, the teachers he liked, and most of his belongings behind.

Adam's aunt and uncle tried to be kind. But they had no children of their own and were not used to having a boy in the house. They treated him as if he were a small child. They watched him all the time. He had to tell them everywhere he went, and they sent him to bed way too early. He couldn't talk things over with them like he could with his parents. He felt very lonely and worried.

If he didn't have the gas mask, Adam might have thought that he had imagined everything.

But the gas mask was real. Adam lifted it from the box and studied it in his bedroom. He even tried it on. He hated the feeling of being closed in. He hated the smell of rubber. How awful it must have been to wear the thing for real!

He wanted to tell someone how awful it had been. But he could not bother his parents now, and he didn't feel Aunt Laura and Uncle Tim would understand. They would either say, "There, there," or laugh at his weird story. If he showed them the gas mask, they might think he stole it.

The only person who could help him at all was Jade Green. After all, she had been there with him. He decided to keep the key and talk to Jade.

Could he get her to look at the supply closet with him?

Adam slept badly that night.

But the next morning, he couldn't wait to go to school. He knew where Jade lived and planned to walk past her house. All at once she was there, in her neat school uniform.

She was just crossing the street in front of him. But her friend Sophie was with her and the two of them were chatting together.

Adam was too shy to say anything to Jade.

It was only during lunch time that he found Jade alone. Then he showed her the key and asked if she had ever been inside the supply closet.

When she said no, Adam didn't believe her. After all, she'd met him in the strange school hall yesterday and gone to the air-raid shelter with him.

"What about the secret room?" he asked her.

Jade laughed. "Oh, that? Well, let's just say it's only gossip."

"All right, but what about the gas mask you gave me? Where did that come from?"

"Gas mask? I don't know what you're talking about," said Jade.

"Yes, you do," said Adam. "I've got it here. It's in my bag. I couldn't leave it at my aunt's in case she found it."

Jade stared at Adam. What was he talking about?

"You must have me mixed up with someone else. I've never given you anything," said Jade.

"Look, there's no need to pretend," said Adam. "I'm not going to tell a teacher or anything. We're in this together. I'm just trying to figure it out, and you're not making it easy for me. If I show you the gas mask . . ."

Adam began to open his school bag, but Jade turned away. She wouldn't even look.

"I don't tell lies!" she snapped. "And I certainly wouldn't give a present to just anyone."

Jade tossed her head and went off to find Sophie.

Now Adam was really upset.

If Jade would not help him,
he would never be able to solve
the puzzle.

Adam thought about his problem
all afternoon. In the end he knew what
to do. He would say nothing more to
anyone. He would hide the gas mask
in the supply closet behind a pile of
books and try to forget all about it.
Nothing was worth all this worry. He
had too many problems already.

Yet Adam soon found that he
couldn't get rid of his problem
that easily.

Chapter 4

The Silver Monster

The next day, Adam hid again in the boys' bathroom after school. Then he crept into the hall when everyone except Mrs. Yates was gone.

By this time, Adam couldn't wait to get rid of the gas mask. All day it had worried him. He felt as if he were carrying a ticking bomb around in his bag. He had weird fears that he was mixed up in something evil, like a wizard's magic spell.

With a shaking hand, he unlocked the closet door and stepped inside. Again the light came on. This time, he made sure to leave the door open.

First, he moved a pile of books to one side. Then he lifted the gas mask from his bag and pushed it into the gap he made. He piled some books in front of it.

As Adam stepped back to make sure the box was well hidden, his foot knocked the edge of the door. Before he could do anything to stop it, the door slammed shut behind him, just as it had the day before.

Adam didn't panic the last time because he knew he had the key safely in his hand. But this time, although he had the key, he was really afraid.

The thing he feared most had happened — he was trapped inside again! Now he had to do something about his problem after all. What would he find when he opened that door again?

He had to open it. He couldn't stay here in the dark all night. And Aunt Laura said she would take him to the hospital that evening to see his parents for the first time since the accident. He had waited a long time for this. He wasn't going to miss it now.

Adam gave the door a push to see if it would open, but it was locked. He had to use the key. He stepped out of the closet in terror. He was afraid to look around.

His most awful fears had come true.

He was back in the mystery hall
again, with the two old posters and the
black curtains.

Adam felt sick. He slumped to
the floor and sat there with his back
against the wall. He didn't dare move.
Then, all at once, there was Jade Green
again, walking toward him in her
shabby dress and sweater. This time
she wasn't carrying a gas mask.

"Do you want to come and see the
barrage balloon?" she asked. "I know
we're not allowed to go there, but we
can hide behind the bushes at the
edge of the field. They've got it on the
ground today, which doesn't happen
very often."

Adam sat there, staring at her. He
felt stupid.

"What's going on?" he asked. "I wish someone would just tell me what's going on."

Jade laughed. "War's going on, silly! But that doesn't mean we can't have a little fun. Come on!"

She held out her arms and dragged Adam to his feet.

Adam was pleased to see Jade. Now he was no longer alone in this strange world. Nothing really bad could happen if the two of them stayed together. So he followed her across the playground and onto the soccer field. One end of it had become a vegetable garden with neat rows of cabbages, carrots, and potatoes.

How strange!

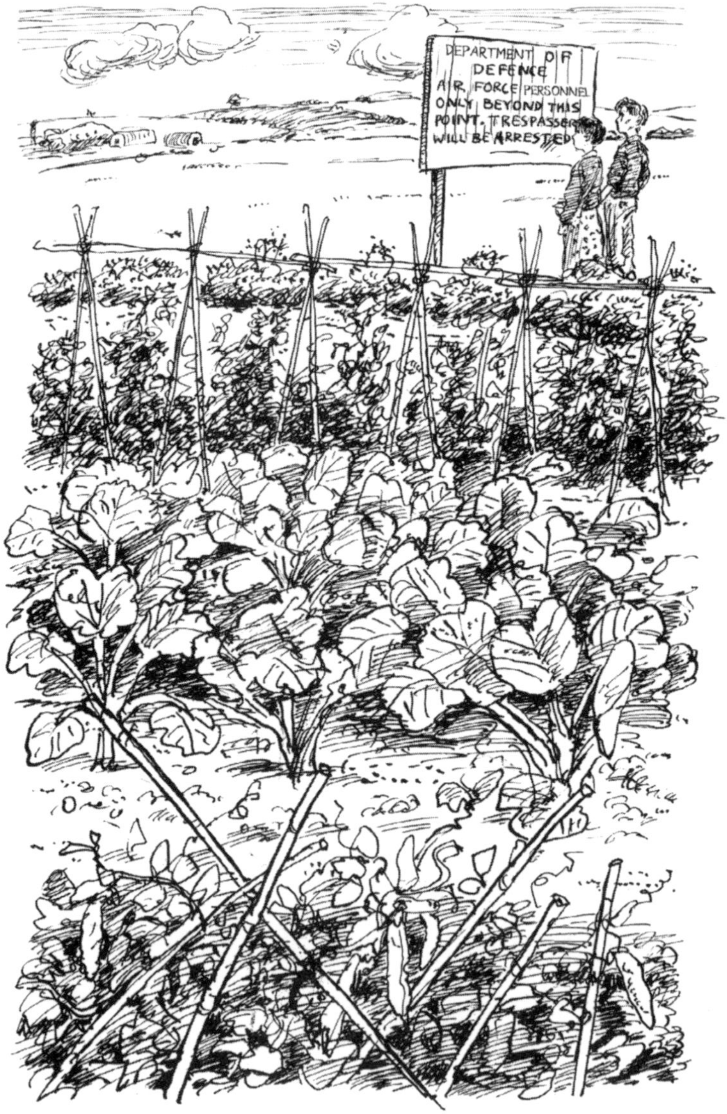
DEPARTMENT OF
DEFENCE
AIR FORCE PERSONNEL
ONLY BEYOND THIS
POINT. TRESPASSERS
WILL BE ARRESTED

The goalpost was gone, and in its place was a huge sign saying in bold, red letters:

DEPARTMENT OF DEFENSE.

AIR FORCE PERSONNEL ONLY

BEYOND THIS POINT.

TRESPASSERS WILL BE ARRESTED.

There were only fields behind the sign. Far away Adam could see a group of huts. Men in light-blue uniforms moving around a great, silver monster, which seemed to be tied to the ground with ropes.

"Look at that!" cried Jade. "Isn't she a beauty? And it's our lucky day. They've taken her down for repairs, so we'll be able to see her up close."

"That's a barrage balloon?" Adam had to admit it was a wonderful sight.

"What did you think it was?" said Jade. "Come on. We can get closer if we slip through these bushes."

"But there's barbed wire."

"It's not so bad down here. We can crawl underneath it. Just keep your head down and be careful."

"But it says 'Trespassers will be arrested'," said Adam.

"Only if they catch us. Anyway, that means grown-ups like German spies. No one's going to bother with kids like us. We're finding and learning new things. They should be pleased with us," said Jade.

Adam didn't want to lose sight of Jade, so he did what she said.

The two managed to slip safely under the bushes. They ran across two fields. They were creeping along one side of the metal fence around the balloon site when the air-raid siren went off.

Chapter 5

Casualty

This time they were caught in the open. Jade knew that the school's air-raid shelters were far away. All the same, she started to run across the fields toward them. She didn't care now whether she was seen or not.

"Come on! We've got to get to the shelters quick!" she called to Adam.

"Can't we use those huts instead?"

"No! They'd be really angry at us!"

"You said they wouldn't mind because we're only kids," said Adam.

"Oh, stop it! Just follow me!"

Adam sprinted after her. What else could he do? But he wasn't looking where he was going. His foot stuck in a hole, and he crashed to the ground.

Now he was really scared. He called after Jade, but she didn't hear him. She just kept on running.

Adam got to his feet. His ankle hurt, but he decided it wasn't too bad. He was just about to try running again when a plane zoomed in.

It made an awful noise as it swooped low over the fields. It was so low that Adam could see the pilot's head in a black helmet and goggles.

Then the plane flew up again
and something dark dropped toward
the ground.

A bomb?

The bomb exploded like thunder
as it hit the ground. A shower of dirt,
stones, bushes, and even a whole
tree were flung into the air. A huge
hole opened up, and the nearby field
vanished into it.

Adam threw himself to the ground.
Something hit him on the side of the
head. He heard an awful scream from
somewhere in front of him. He looked
up in terror. He was just in time to see
Jade Green's body tossed into the air
before it fell like a rag doll into the
huge hole the bomb had made. Then
it lay still.

Chapter 6

Missing Person

Adam Belman opened his eyes. He was in a hospital bed and a nurse was bending over him.

"I think he's awake now," she was telling someone. Then she began to explain to Adam where he was. "You're going to be fine," she told him in a gentle voice.

Adam moved his legs and arms one by one. Everything seemed to be there, but his head hurt.

He couldn't remember anything. That was bad. What had happened? He tried to think back and then he remembered the air raid. He must have been hurt. All at once he could see that huge hole in the ground opening in front of him. He could see Jade Green being thrown into the air and then falling into the hole.

He turned his head and asked the nurse, "Is Jade all right?"

"Jade?"

"Jade Green, the girl who was with me," said Adam.

"No one was with you, dear, as far as I know. But your aunt's on the way, so perhaps she can tell you what happened."

When Aunt Laura came she began to explain what had happened to him.

"Don't you remember, dear?" said his aunt. "Mrs. Yates, the school custodian, locked you in the supply closet. She didn't know you were in there, of course.

"When you didn't come home, I called the school, and they searched around until they found you. You had blacked out. The doctor says it's nothing to worry about. It may even have something to do with your car accident, or you might have banged your head on one of the closet shelves. There's a bump on the side of your head."

"I was hit by a rock," said Adam.

Aunt Laura looked puzzled. "Well, never mind, dear! It's all over now. They want to keep you in the hospital for one more night to make sure you're all right, then you can come home."

"She's dead, isn't she?" asked Adam.

Aunt Laura looked worried. "No one's dead, dear, and you're going to be fine. You're in the same hospital as your mom and dad. So your mom will come and see you soon. And before you go home you'll be able to visit your dad in the wing down the hall. Won't that be great?"

"But what about the air raid? Why won't anyone talk about it?" asked Adam.

"Air raid?" It was clear that Aunt Laura didn't know what Adam was talking about. She was growing more and more worried.

"It was awful, Aunt Laura! But what I really want to know is if Jade's all right. Maybe there's a different ward for girls. Could you find out for me, please? It's very important," Adam told her.

"Don't you worry about anyone else," Aunt Laura replied. "Just think about getting better."

Adam tried to sit up.

"But don't you see? I can't get better until I know what's happened to Jade. She was hurt much worse than I was."

As far as Aunt Laura knew, no one else had been hurt. Only Adam. The boy's mind must be confused. However, she could see that it was important to comfort him, even if she had to pretend to believe his story.

She asked the nurse, and then the doctor, what to do. They told her to call the school to ask about Jade.

"He's got this girl on his mind," said the doctor. "Once he knows she's all right and not hurt in any way, maybe he'll calm down."

Aunt Laura did not look very happy. She agreed to make the call, but in an odd way she felt afraid of what she might find out.

Chapter 7

Jade the Third

Aunt Laura phoned the school right away. A little later, Jade Green walked into the room with Adam's uncle. Jade was carrying a huge bunch of flowers.

Adam sat up in bed, looking better already.

"Are you okay?" he asked Jade. He was amazed. He thought she was dead or badly hurt.

Jade looked just as puzzled as everyone else.

"I'm sorry about what happened to you," she told Adam. "Here are some flowers and I hope you get better soon. But I don't see where I fit into all this. I'm here because your uncle told me you were worried about me being hurt. But as you can see, I'm fine."

"Don't you remember the air raid?" asked Adam.

Jade's face lit up. Now she knew what Adam was talking about.

"You mean the air raid Mr. Evans was telling us about in class? You must have been thinking about my granddad's sister!" she said.

Jade started to explain to the grown-ups what she had told her class. She had talked about her great-aunt during the lesson on World War II.

"She was called Jade Green, like me. I was named after her and I even look like she did at my age. Mr. Evans was telling us about an air raid that happened during World War II near our school. I said that was when my great-aunt had been killed. Mr. Evans asked if it would upset me to talk about it, but I said no. So I stood up in class and described what had happened, the way my granddad has often told it to me."

"On the day of the raid, when the siren sounded, all the other children marched into the shelters. But Great-Aunt Jade had gone off somewhere on her own. She said she wanted to get a closer look at the barrage balloon which was kept in some fields behind the school."

"I know! I was there! I saw her!" shouted Adam.

"Don't be silly. You couldn't have!" laughed Jade. "That was way back in 1942. I think that knock on your head confused you. You got mixed up with what you heard in class."

"That's where you're wrong," cried Adam, "because the gas mask was real! The one you gave me, remember? I even tried it on!"

He wanted to make everyone believe him.

Jade gave a sad little smile.

"Oh yes, I talked about the gas mask, too. Great-Aunt Jade left hers behind in school that day, something the children were told never to do."

"The school kept it in memory of her," she continued. "I believe it's still around on a shelf at the back of the supply closet."

Slowly, very slowly, Adam began putting together the pieces of this weird story. He was still trying to make some sense of it when something amazing happened.

A woman walked into the ward carrying a small, white bundle.

"Mom!" cried Adam and almost jumped out of bed.

Adam's mom handed the bundle to Aunt Laura, then ran to hug her son.

"Oh, Adam, it's so good to see you! And Dad's coming to visit you soon."

"He's better now," his mom continued. "He'll be walking again in a week or so."

They hugged each other as if they would never let go. Then Adam's mom took her bundle from Aunt Laura and held it out to Adam.

"Meet your new little sister," she said proudly.

Adam stared down at the tiny face and the tiny fingers. And all at once the problems and secrets of the past didn't seem important anymore. Now there was this wonderful new hope for the future.

"What shall we call her?" his mom asked. "Any ideas?"

"Why don't we call her Jade?" said
Adam happily.

And that seemed to please everyone.

About the Author

Hazel Townson began her writing career as a poet. When a magazine sent her some children's books to review, she decided to start writing her own children's books.

She became an author and a librarian, eventually quitting her librarian job to write full-time. Besides writing, Hazel travels around Great Britain talking to children at schools and libraries.

Glossary

air raid (AIR RADE)—an attack by armed airplanes

barrage balloon (buh-RAHJ buh-LOON)—a special, large balloon used to support wires or nets as protection against air attacks

bunker (BUNG-kur)—a protective underground room

clutter (CLUH-tur)—scattered and disorganized objects

gas mask (GASS MASK)—a mask used to protect the face and lungs from harmful vapors

gossip (GAH-sip)—information that is passed from one person to the next

siren (SYE-ruhn)—a loud warning sound

trespasser (TRESS-pass-ur)—a person who goes onto someone else's property without permission

wing (WING)—a section of a building

Discussion Questions

1. At the beginning of the story, Adam thought World War II was boring. How do you think he felt about the war after his experiences? Explain your answer.

2. Adam kept thinking that as long as Jade was around, he was sure nothing terrible would happen. Why did Adam trust Jade so much?

4. Do you think Adam actually went back in time? Or do you think it was all a dream? Why?

Writing Prompts

1. When Adam went into the supply closet, he traveled back in time to World War II. Write about a time in history you would like to visit. What would you want to see? Who would you want to meet? Explain.

2. During an air raid, the school children ran for shelter to the underground bunkers. Write how you would feel if you were hiding inside a bunker during an attack.

3. Imagine that Adam decided to go back to the supply closet one more time. Write about what you think would happen.

Internet Sites

Do you want to know more about subjects related to this book? Or are you interested in learning about other topics? Then check out FactHound, a fun, easy way to find Internet sites.

Our investigative staff has already sniffed out great sites for you!

Here's how to use FactHound:

1. Visit *www.facthound.com*

2. Select your grade level.

3. To learn more about subjects related to this book, type in the book's ISBN number: **1598890034**.

4. Click the **Fetch It** button.

FactHound will fetch the best Internet sites for you!